SUPER
GABBA FRIENDS!

ADAPTED BY TINA GALLO
BASED ON THE SCREENPLAY WRITTEN BY CHRISTIAN JACOBS,
EVAN DORKIN & SARAH DYER
ILLUSTRATED BY PARKER JACOBS

Ready-to-Read

SIMON SPOTLIGHT
New York   London   Toronto   Sydney   New Delhi

SIMON SPOTLIGHT An imprint of Simon & Schuster Children's Publishing Division 1230 Avenue of the Americas, New York, New York 10020
Based on on the TV series Yo Gabba Gabba! ™ as seen on Nick Jr.™
Yo Gabba Gabba! TM & © 2013 GabbaCaDabra LLC. All rights reserved, including the right of reproduction in whole or inpart in any form.
SIMON SPOTLIGHT, READY-TO-READ, and colophon are registered trademarks of Simon & Schuster.
For information about special discounts for bulk purchases, please contact Simon & Schuster Special Sales at 1-866-506-1949 or business@simonandschuster.com.
Manufactured in the United States of America 1112 LAK First Edition 2 4 6 8 10 9 7 5 3 1
ISBN 978-1-4424-6184-0 ISBN 978-1-4424-6247-2 (eBook)

It is quiet in Gabba Land.

Everyone is bored.

"Let's play superheroes!"
Toodee says.

"How do we play?" Foofa asks.

"Imagine your superpower,"
Toodee says.
"Then tell us what it is."

Plex says, "I am Ultra-Plex. I can fly really high!"

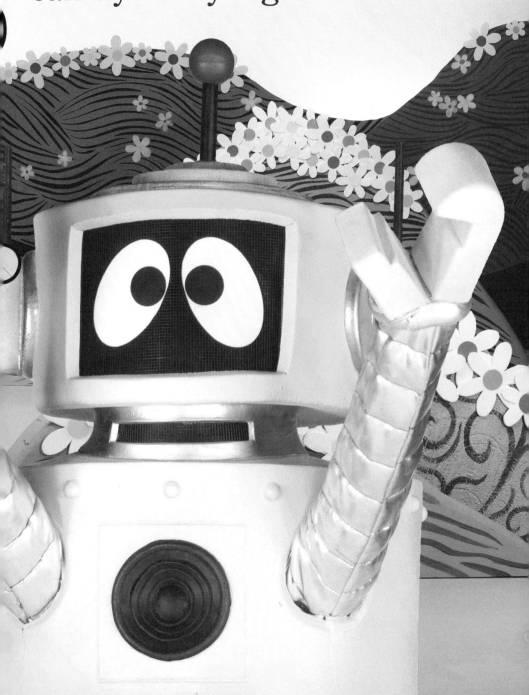

"I am Amazing Toodee.
I am superstrong!
I can lift polar bears
all day long!"

"Captain Muno is my name.
I can run really fast
and save the day!"

"Incredible Brobee is who
I am! I can stretch my arms
across Gabba Land!"

"I am Fantastic Foofa!
I like plants.
My superpower is to make
them dance!"

"Now we all are superheroes!" Muno says.

Then Plex has
an idea.

"It would be even better if we were a superhero team!"

Hey, we are superheroes.

We are supergreat!

Making things better, super-teamwork!

"We need a name for our superteam," Brobee says.

"The Super Gabba Friends!"
Muno says.

"Hooray!"

All the Super Gabba
Friends cheer!